Mum and Dad said it was
**very exciting.**

But Daisy wasn't excited at all.
She was **worried.**

Our Emotions and Behaviour

# But What If?

Written by Sue Graves

Illustrated by

Desideria Guicciardini

WATTS

N · SYDNEY

Mum, Dad and Daisy were moving to a new house. Daisy was going to a new school, too.

**What if** she didn't like the new house? And **what if** the neighbours were mean?

Daisy was also worried about her cat, Tigger.

What if Tigger **didn't like** the new house? What if he ran away?

Daisy worried about her new school, too. She liked Miss Lane, her teacher. What if her new teacher **wasn't nice?**

And what if she didn't make any new friends? Daisy was **very worried.**

One night, Mum and Dad went out. Grandpa came to look after Daisy. But when it was bedtime, Daisy couldn't sleep.

12

She told Grandpa about the new house.
She told him all her worries.

Then Grandpa said that when he was a boy, he worried about lots of things. He said he worried that he wasn't as tall as his friends.

Daisy laughed. Grandpa was very tall. He was just as tall as Dad.

Grandpa said, "It's easy to worry about new things or big changes. And even if one or two of your worries come true at first, someone will be there to help you **solve the problem.**"

Grandpa said it was silly to worry about something that **might never happen.** He said it was better to look on the bright side.

Grandpa said Daisy might **love** her new house. Her new neighbours might be **really nice.**

Grandpa said Daisy's new school might be **even better** than her old one. Her new teacher might be **even nicer** than Miss Lane.

He said he thought she would make lots of **new friends,** too.
Daisy felt **much better**.

Then Grandpa said he did not believe Tigger would ever run away. He said Tigger loved Daisy too much to do that!

Daisy felt **much, much better.**

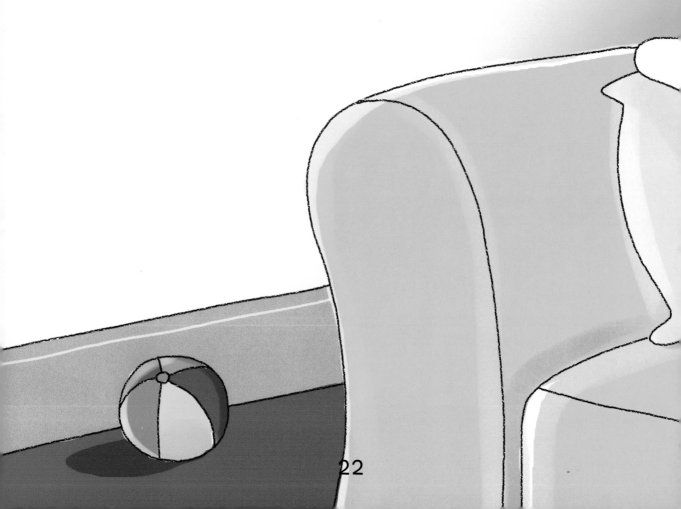

Daisy went to bed. She fell
fast asleep. Best of all, she
didn't feel worried anymore!

25

# Can you tell the story of Harry going to his friend's birthday party?

How do you think Harry felt when he arrived?

How do you think Harry felt after he met his friend?

# A note about sharing this book

The *Our Emotions and Behaviour* series has been developed to provide a starting point for further discussion on children's feelings and behaviour, both in relation to themselves and to other people.

## But What If?
This story explores, in a reassuring way, some of the typical worries that children may experience. It also points out that different things worry different people and that not everyone worries about the same things.

The book aims to encourage children to have a developing awareness of their own needs, views and feelings, and to be sensitive to the needs, views and feelings of others.

## Storyboard puzzle
The wordless storyboard on pages 26 and 27 provides an opportunity for speaking and listening. Children are encouraged to tell the story illustrated in the panels: Harry is worried about going to his friend's birthday party. He is worried that he won't know many people. But he soon sees his friend and has fun joining in with the party games.

## How to use the book
The book is designed for adults to share with either an individual child or a group of children, and as a starting point for discussion.

The book also provides visual support and repeated words and phrases to build confidence in children who are starting to read on their own.

## Before reading the story
Choose a time to read when you and the children are relaxed and have time to share the story.

Spend time looking at the illustrations and talk about what the book may be about before reading it together.

**After reading, talk about the book with the children:**

- What was the story about? Have any of the children ever moved house? How did they feel? Were they worried about living in a new neighbourhood? Were they worried about sleeping in a different bedroom? Were they worried that they might find it hard to make new friends and were they upset at leaving old friends behind? Invite the children to tell you how they resolved their worries and who helped them. Ask if any of their worries turned out to be unfounded.

  Encourage the children to talk about their experiences.

- Extend this conversation by talking about other things that worry the children. Take the opportunity to point out that different things worry different people and that not everyone worries about the same things.

- Now talk about things that might worry adults. Again, point out that adults worry about different things. Similarly point out that adults also worried about things when they were children. If appropriate, illustrate this with an example from your own childhood, e.g. feeling worried about going to school for the first time or about trying a new activity.

- Look at the end of the story again. Daisy felt much better after she shared her worries with Grandpa. Talk about the benefits of sharing a worry with someone children know and trust.

- Look at the storyboard puzzle. Ask the children to talk about Harry's worries about going to the party. What is he worrying about? How does seeing his friend help him overcome his worries?

Suggest that children draw pictures of people they would confide in if they felt worried.

First published in 2013 by
Franklin Watts
338 Euston Road
London
NW1 3BH

Franklin Watts Australia
Level 17/207 Kent Street
Sydney
NSW 2000

Text © Franklin Watts 2013
Illustrations © Desideria Guicciardini 2013

The rights of Sue Graves to be identified as the author
and Desideria Guicciardini as the illustrator of this Work have
been asserted in accordance with the Copyright, Designs
and Patents Act, 1988.

A CIP catalogue record for this book is available
from the British Library.

ISBN 978 1 4451 1623 5

Editor: Jackie Hamley
Designer: Peter Scoulding

Printed in China

Franklin Watts is a division of
Hachette Children's Books,
an Hachette UK company.
www.hachette.co.uk